Dear Gerard and Shane
from Grandma with love.

A Pocketful Of
Sunshine

by
Velma Seawell Daniels

illustrated by
Mary O'Keefe Young

The C.R. Gibson Company, Norwalk, CT

EVEN as I grow older, I know I'll never grow up. Not long ago I took a six-year-old friend to an amusement park. Together we rode the merry-go-round and the Ferris wheel and the roller coaster. We ate foot-long hot dogs and cotton candy and drank pink lemonade. When I suggested that she have her face painted like a clown, she said she would if I would. So we did.

Later, after I had dropped her off at her home and was in the kitchen making supper, my husband came in from work. Shock spread over his face when he was greeted by a grinning clown. Then he laughed and said, "You look like the happiest kid on the block."

And right then, I was.

Happiness is a habit—cultivate it!
Elbert Hubbard

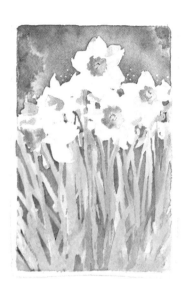

Happiness is what you are,
Not what you have;
What you give,
Not what you get;
Not what somebody does for you,
But what you do for somebody else.

Winston K. Pendleton

TWO letters came in the mail this morning. One, in reply to a letter I had written four or five months ago, began, "Please excuse me for taking so long to answer your last letter but you have no idea how busy...." I was glad to hear from my friend, but I was a bit intimidated by all the trouble she went through to write to me.

The second letter was so short I am quoting it in full. It read, "Your letter that came yesterday was like opening a Christmas present early. I feel like a pancake with honey poured all over it. Thank you so much."

As I enjoyed the warmth of my friend's hasty note, I recognized the truth in the old saying, "It's not so much what you say as how you say it."

LITTLE five-year-old Mallory and her grandmother saw a lot of each other. They lived only half a block apart, and whether you called it babysitting or merely visiting, Mallory rarely missed a day at Grandma's.

When she entered kindergarten, she would entertain her grandmother with her big scratch pad and box full of colored felt pens. "This is what I learned today," she would say, as she scrawled her ABC's and numbers on her pad. And she never stopped talking. She delighted in repeating the stories that had been read to her— enriched and embellished with new twists and turns from her own little imagination.

Then one day her grandmother asked Mallory, "What do you want to be when you grow up?"

Mallory, faced with a question she had never thought about before, sat silently for a few moments then looked up at her grandmother and said, "I don't want to be anything when I grow up. I don't have to be anything. I love you and you love me—that's enough!"

Believe in people!
Believe that behind every doorway
of every house you pass,
someone is
cooking a fluffy souffle,
sketching a new fashion,
composing a symphony,
writing a poem,
sculpturing a masterpiece,
painting a portrait,
working on a novel,
striving to be what God wants them to be.

THE popular sport of soaring or sailplaning or gliding or whatever you want to call it attracts pilots to Central Florida from all over the world. They come for camaraderie and competition in various events.

Sailplanes are sleek little airplanes, usually single seaters, with no engines. They are launched by conventional aircraft that take them with a tow-rope to about 3,000 feet.

There they disconnect their towrope and are released, as one pilot said to me, "Into the hands of God, where you soar among His clouds, and where you're kept aloft by His air currents which ebb and flow to His will. I've never known a richer experience than when I trust Him with my life, sitting in my tiny plane alone in the sky."

I often think about that man and what he said. And how much richer we would be if we would dare to disconnect our worldly towrope and put ourselves in God's hands and trust Him to see that our own tiny ship is kept aloft.

If I take the wings of the morning, and dwell in the uttermost parts of the sea; even there shall thy hand lead me, and thy right hand shall hold me.

Psalm 139: 9-10

THIS morning I re-read one of the most heartening passages from the Bible, Deuteronomy 28:1-2. Moses spoke these words more than 3400 years ago to tell his followers of the great promise given to them by God.

This is what he said: "The Lord thy God will set thee on high above all nations of the earth: And all these blessings shall come on thee, and overtake thee, if thou shalt hearken unto the voice of the Lord thy God."

Who could ask for a greater promise than that? What a cheerful thought to start my day!

Jesus Gave Three Cheers!

The Cheer Of Forgiveness
Be of good cheer; thy sins be forgiven thee.
Matthew 9:2

The Cheer Of Courage
Be of good cheer; it is I; be not afraid.
Matthew 14:27

The Cheer Of Victory
Be of good cheer; I have overcome the world.
John 16:33

WE had come to our beach cottage for a weekend of rest and loosening up. This was our last night before heading for home, and as usual, I decided to take one of my night-walks before going to bed. When I stepped outside, I was greeted by the full moon, brighter than I could ever remember it. So bright it was, that as I walked toward the beach I could read the For Sale sign on the lot next door. When I reached the top of the sand dune and looked out over the gulf, I couldn't take another step. For there in front of me, a shimmery, golden path stretched across the water all the way to the moon. There was no wind, there was no surf, nor was there any sound. There was nothing except the golden picture before me—the picture of perfect tranquility, painted it seemed, just for me by the hand of God.

I don't remember how long I stood there, in His presence, dazed by His artistry. But as I turned back toward the cottage, I remembered to say, *"Thank you, dear God, for giving me these moments of tranquility. Thank you, dear Lord, for showing me once again just how beautiful your world really is."*

THE low slanting rays of the early morning sun flood my living room. Another spring day crying for me to open up and let it come inside.

I rush to respond and fling the doors wide. Before me stands a living greeting card—the dogwood waving their hands "hello" and the magnolias vying for my attention with their haunting perfume.

Dawn and dogwood! May and magnolias! God's way of saying, "Have a cheerful day!"

Joy is not in things, it is in us.
Richard Wagner

*A good natured man has the whole world to be
happy out of.*
Alexander Pope

*So of cheerfulness or a good temper, the more of it
is spent, the more of it remains.*
Ralph Waldo Emerson

SOME people have a gift for making each and every child feel special, no matter what his or her achievement level is. Miss Giles is such a person. It was the first rehearsal for the Tiny Angels Bell Choir, and Miss Giles had volunteered to teach the little group of six to nine year olds. Her technique was simple. She merely pointed to each child when it was time for that particular bell.

All was going well except for Horace. He was six years old, and he was the smallest. Horace stood on the end holding the little High-G bell. There was only one spot for him in the simple little tune they were learning, and he kept missing his cue.

Finally, Miss Giles took him aside and whispered something to him. After that, she would point to him first. He would raise his tiny bell and give her a dinner bell type ring, "tingle-ling, tingle-ling," for a count of five. He would do it again when she pointed to him at the end of the tune.

On the way home after the rehearsal, his mother asked him if he was sure he wanted to play with the choir the following Sunday.

"Oh," he said. "I have to be there. Miss Giles has given me the most important part. You see, if it wasn't for me, the other kids wouldn't know when to start or when to stop."

Those who bring sunshine to the lives of others
cannot keep it from themselves.
Sir James M. Barrie

"BE good to yourself," said the leader at a retreat I attended recently. "Start your day auspiciously. Begin it with a "prayer walk." It will stimulate your appetite for life. You'll be exercising close to heaven.

It goes like this. As the sun begins to show its face and drive away the gloom of night, ask God to guide your footsteps through your neighborhood. And as you pass each house along the way, hesitate for just a bit and say a prayer for those inside. *"Please, dear God, bless this day for them. Lead them through your paths of righteousness. Protect them from evil. Let them know that this is the day that you have made for them so that they might rejoice and be glad in it."*

And so you go, walking quietly through town, living a twenty-thirty-forty-minute morning prayer for others, then, finding on your own doorstep when you return the greatest gift of all, yours for the day: the peace of God, which passeth all understanding.

So now on good days, I take my prayer walk outdoors and on rainy days, I take it in my mind. And I always return refreshed, at peace and ready for the day.

MY husband and I waited for an overcast day to undertake our annual back-breaking chore of scraping the barnacles from the bottom of our small fishing boat. Together we pulled it out of the water and turned it bottom side up on two saw-horses so that we could work without bending over. Barnacles, as everyone who lives near the sea knows, are pesky shellfish that attach themselves to rocks and pilings and, in our case, to the bottom of the boat.

On this particular day the work went well. Armed with paint scrapers and cold chisels, and reinforced with a pitcher of iced tea, the task was done in less than two hours, including the final rubdown with steel wool.

As we righted the boat and slid it back into the water, my husband said, "We did a nice job this time, and it wasn't too hard, either. Remember the first time we did it, when we had let the barnacles grow and spread for three years? It took us two whole days. That was really a killer. I guess barnacles are like bad habits. Once they get a solid hold on you—they can be killers. But if you keep scraping on them often enough, they never get the upper hand."

WHILE I was still a little girl, my grandmother taught me many of the great spiritual truths that have so enriched my life. From her I came to understand the certainty of God's love and faith as opposed to the love of material possessions.

She and my grandfather lived in a two story colonial type house at the edge of town; a haven for her children and grandchildren. I enjoyed the times when I was allowed to "sleep over" and the afternoons when I helped her with quilting. "Help" meant watching while she stitched. "Eleven stitches to the inch," she used to say. "They have to be just right. A proper quilt will last for generations."

I dreamed of someday owning the one she had promised me, with the traditional Double Wedding Ring pattern. But that was not to be.

One windy winter night a fire destroyed their home and everything in it, including the quilt that someday was to have been mine.

The next day my grandparents knelt in the ashes and thanked God for sparing them and giving them a chance to start again.

She said, "All we lost were things. Nothing else—not love or courage or determination or anything that gives value to living. Just things, my child. I can always piece another quilt."

NO one but you, my exuberant and fast-thinking friend, could have turned our possible embarrassment into a social triumph.

You had written me that you would be in town for the Christmas ball, and that the dress you would be wearing was, "as colorful as a tropical bird's plumage." I could hardly wait to see you dressed in the latest fashion from Palm Beach. The best I could find was a bright little number from our local small town emporium.

Then came the big night. As my husband and I walked into the ballroom, there you stood in the bright lights near the orchestra—wearing a dress exactly like mine. We saw each other at the same instant. And it was in that instant that you showed such great presence of mind. You rushed across the dance floor crying out, "There's my twin. There's my twin! I've been waiting for you." Then you grabbed me and turned to face the crowd and cried out, "How do you like us?"

I've thought of that moment many times. How the spotlight was turned on us and how everyone cheered and applauded. When I remember that evening, I remember it with only one regret. You were wearing a size 5 and I was wearing a size 12.

THE haunting beat of the Christmas music from the stereo softened the atmosphere throughout the house—*Pa-rum-pum-pum-pum, rum-pum-pum-pum.*

It was gift wrapping time. Everybody was busy with the fancy paper and ribbons and bows and stickem-tape: Grandmother, who was visiting for Christmas week, Mother, 10-year-old Wendy and her best-friend Martha Jean—and of course, Marc.

This was Marc's first experience with gift wrapping because he was only five. He embraced the idea with enthusiasm and gusto.

What fun! The grownups were wrapping on the dining room table and the children were working in secret in their rooms. Busy, busy— back and forth—borrowing tape and paper and ribbon. The Christmas music always playing.

"*Pa-rum-pum-pum-pum,*" said Grandmother. "That's my favorite this year. I change from time to time, but this year it's *rum-pum-pum-pum!*"

On Christmas morning, under the tree, there sat a rather crudely wrapped package. "From Marc to Grandma," the tag read. And sure enough, when Grandma unwrapped her gift, it was Marc's most prized gift from last Christmas, his little tin drum, *rum-pum-pum-pum*".

DECEMBER is such a rich time of year. It's so full of good cheer, brotherly love, forgiveness, and the celebration of our Savior that some of it should spill over into June, July, January, March, May, August, April, February, October, September and November!

FRIENDS and family members had gathered to honor a couple on their 50th wedding anniversary. At the height of the festivities, the usual cries of "Speech, speech," were heard.

"Yes, it's time for a speech," agreed their minister who was acting as the unofficial toastmaster. Turning to the husband, he said, "Of all the couples I have known, none ever seemed to be enjoying a more perfect marriage than you. Tell us your secret."

The man thought for a moment and said, "There's no big secret. When we first met, we both worked for a large company in Cincinnati. I was in public relations, and she was in sales. Once I decided I wanted to marry her, I treated her as though she were a possible client. Every morning, before she arrived at work, I slipped a gushy little note in the top drawer of her desk. And when she decided she was out to get me, she treated me like a prospective customer.

Every Saturday night when I called on her, she greeted me with a batch of her home-made sugar cookies.

"When we got married, she suggested that if I would continue to treat her like a possible client, she would treat me like a possible customer.

"So for fifty years, I've been writing her a gushy note every day. And if there's any questions about those sugar cookies—you'll notice that I'm about twenty pounds over-weight."

"MY dear, please come by sometime today if you can," said my elderly friend on the phone early one Monday morning.

Of course I said "Yes." I wouldn't say "No," to this dear little lady. But this was a Monday—my busy-busy-busiest day of the week—and an early morning Florida rain promised to stick around all day.

My watch read 4:30 when I finally arrived at her front door. My feet hurt and my back ached from rushing about all day, and my nerves were a bit frayed, too. And dodging in and out of the rain had left me a bit soggy around the edges.

Strangely enough, all of that had slipped from my mind within minutes. A sudden restfulness came over me as I snuggled down in her big easy chair next to her picture window. What had happened to me? Maybe it was her smile and hug when she greeted me or the tea and cookies that appeared almost instantly or maybe just being in her presence.

What did she want to see me about? Nothing in particular. Just to visit. When we had finished a bit of small-talk, she said, "Hasn't it been a beautiful day—this wonderful rain?"

"Wonderful? It's been awful." I said. "All day. It slowed everything down—hard to drive—soaking wet—all that. It wasn't wonderful for me."

"I guess you're right," she said. "While you were in it, I had the pleasure of sitting here all day listening to it. Listen to it now! The rain that runs down the rain spout sort of sets the rhythm. The high notes come when the rain hits the brass mailbox by the door. If you listen carefully, you hear a different tone when it hits the shutters and the window pane and the sidewalk and the leaves and the azaleas. It's like a set of chimes. It's lovely. I call it God's carillon."

When I started home, driving was different than before. No longer tense or harried or agitated, I caught myself humming a soft accompaniment to the rain as it swished in the street and beat against the roof and windows and hood of my car. My wise friend was right. The rain did sound like God's carillon. I just hadn't been listening.

WHEN I asked my friend about her birthday the weekend before, she said, "Super! John took me and the kids to a wonderful restaurant for dinner, and then the kids gave me the nicest present I've ever received. Let me show you."

As she reached in her purse, I expected to see a diamond pin or gold necklace. Instead she handed me a rather large brown prescription bottle. "Read that label," she said.

I did. It read, "From The Kids' Dispensary. Terry, Joe, Alice. Take one daily with love." Inside was what looked like a supply of capsules.

"I don't get it," I said. "I didn't either, at first," she said. "But in each capsule is a note on a tiny strip of paper. Of course, I've only opened three of them so far. But they went like this: Good for one living room vacuuming, signed Alice; Good for one front yard raking, signed Joe; Good for cleaning up the family room, signed Alice. I'm dying to see if Terry has put in one saying she is going to clean up her room." Then she laughed and said. "Look how many there are in there. I'll be enjoying my birthday all year long!"

A joy that's shared is a joy made double.
John Roy

Marry for love not money. If you marry for money—no matter how much you get—you'll be short-changed.

MY ancestor's home, Happy Hollow, still stands in a rural valley among the red clay hills of Georgia.

Even though it hasn't been in the family for years, I drove by last summer just to take a look. There it sat, freshly painted, and exactly like the Happy Hollow I remembered.

What vivid memories! I remember visiting there as a child and listening to my grandfather tell about his boyhood; how his parents farmed the old homestead and how he had to do his daily chores—milking the cows, churning butter, gathering eggs, feeding the livestock, and chopping wood for the kitchen stove.

I particularly remembered him telling me how Happy Hollow got its name. "Usually on a Sunday afternoon," he said, "we'd have quite a gathering here, what with uncles and aunts and cousins and a few friends. So, one time when everybody was here, Mama—that would be your great-grandmother—said we ought to have a name for our farm. She said it ought to be a happy name so that everybody up and down the hollow would know this was a happy and contented household.

"She said, 'Everybody think of a name.' And the funniest thing happened. Everybody shouted out at once, Happy Hollow! Maybe that's why it has always been such a joy to live here."

Whatever it was—the name, the peace of the valley, or maybe the love that my relatives had for each other—some of it rubbed off on me—and stuck—and has made my memories of Happy Hollow joyful.

Where your pleasure is, there is your treasure;
Where your treasure, there your heart;
Where your heart, there your happiness.
St. Augustine

A jade green Chinese ginger jar sits in my foyer, filled with gilded lotus leaves, a gift from a dear friend.

She explained that the lotus is sacred to the people of Egypt, India and China, and that gilding the leaves is an ancient and one-time secret craft. "On several trips to the Orient," she told me, "I became acquainted with a horticultur-ist who arranged for me to take lessons in gather-ing, preserving, gilding and arranging lotus leaves, bamboo and other native grasses.

"Then, several years ago, I was given permission to gather some of the leaves from an Oriental water garden here in Florida. Only perfect leaves, free of bug bites or bruises were selected, and the time had to be exact, when the leaves were a certain shade of olive green. It took three gardeners, wading in waist-deep murky water, four hours to gather my leaves.

"The process of preparing the leaves was slow and tedious. It took four years of drying, curing, and preserving before I could even begin to add the decorative gilt."

That was more than fifteen years ago, and the leaves sparkle and gleam in their ginger jar as brightly today as the day my friend put them there.

When I think of the time and perseverance she put into her handiwork, I'm reminded of something that the great Quaker, William Penn said, "Patience and diligence, like faith, remove mountains."

WHEN out-of-state guests visit, we often take them on a day's sightseeing trip that includes a tour of the Kennedy Space Center at Cape Canaveral.

No matter how many times I visit the Cape, I come away with a fresh feeling of awe and wonderment. In my mind, I sit next to those men in the top of that huge rocket waiting for the countdown.

I think of the thousands of bits and pieces that have been brought together to make the space ship and its boosters, each in its exact place—each doing its appointed task. I think of the workers, scattered across the country, whose hands have made those parts and of the men and women who later assembled them.

I marvel at the scientists and engineers and technicians who made the whole thing work; who understood how God's universe works and were able to plot the course of the ship through outer space.

Yes, when I think of the astronauts waiting confidently for "ignition and lift-off," I can understand what the great Greek poet Homer said some 2700 years ago, "By mutual confidence and mutual aid great deeds are done, and great discoveries made."

DEAR God,
Thank you for not expecting me:
      to sing
      to preach
      to paint
      to farm

You gave those talents to:
      my neighbor
      my pastor
      my husband
      my uncle

You gave me the gift of appreciation
for all of them.
                    Amen

TODAY I saw the simple act of love.

As we were enjoying breakfast overlooking the lake, three sleek, dark brown otters swimming with the grace of Olympic stars, headed for the shore. Slinking up on the sandy beach, they awkwardly flip-flopped onto our neighbor's dock. The smallest of the three, obviously a cub, spied the steps leading to the upper deck over the boathouse. He slithered up the first three steps as quickly as lightning. But before he could climb any higher, papa otter reached up and slapped him down.

Otters love to romp and play, but in this case papa otter wasn't in a mood for nonsense. The mother bounced across the deck, shaking her head and watching with great interest. Several times, the little fellow tried to climb the steps. Each time, "whack," he was slapped down.

Finally, the cub seemed to get the message and stretched out on the dock to rest in the sunshine. Right away, papa and mama slid over to the cub and cradled him in their paws and nuzzled him close to them.

Yes, today I saw a perfect demonstration of family unity reinforced and strengthened by the power of discipline and love.

BLESS you, my tiny little white flower, for doing
your job so well. Maybe you don't know what
I'm talking about so I'll tell you.

Late one night when my husband and I returned
from a trip, your "welcome home" nearly over-
whelmed us. "That night-blooming Jasmine sure
is out tonight, isn't it?" he said.

Then, as long-married couples so often do,
we spoke together as one voice, "That sure
brings back memories, doesn't it?"

He chuckled softly and turned and put his
arms around me and hugged me and whispered,
"Yes, it does. It surely does."

What memories were those little flower? Ah, a
night long ago, a place far from here, and another
Jasmine filling the air with her fragrance. Two
young lovers strolling hand in hand in the moon-
light, chatting happily about their plans for their
wedding day. Thank you for those memories.

WHEN you leave my studio-workroom through the outside door, you step directly onto a cobblestone path that leads to my reflecting pool.

It's not a big pool—about six by eight feet, kidney shaped, rock-lined, and only eighteen inches deep. Close beside it sits a small wrought iron seat. The shade of a willow, across the pool, turns the whole place into a cozy hideaway.

I come here usually in the late afternoon when I'm tired. I come alone, except of course for Chantilly, my tiny kitten. She likes to sit in my lap, sometimes napping, sometimes purring, and occasionally fanning her paw at a passing insect.

This is my place for relaxation, reflection and renewal—a place to sit and think and dream and plan, a place for quiet meditation, a place where I can heed the voice of the Lord as he speaks in the 46th Psalm, "Be still, and know that I am God."

Book design by Mary O'Keefe Young
Type set in ITC Garamond